Bedtime at Aunt Carmen's

Written by Carrie Nicholson

Illustrated by Darcia Labrosse

Silver Burdett Ginn
A Division of Simon & Schuster
160 Gould Street
Needham Heights, MA 02194-2310

Design and production by Bill SMITH STUDIO

ISBN: 0-663-61723-5 Silver Burdett Ginn

3 4 5 6 7 8 9 10 SP 01 00 99 98 97

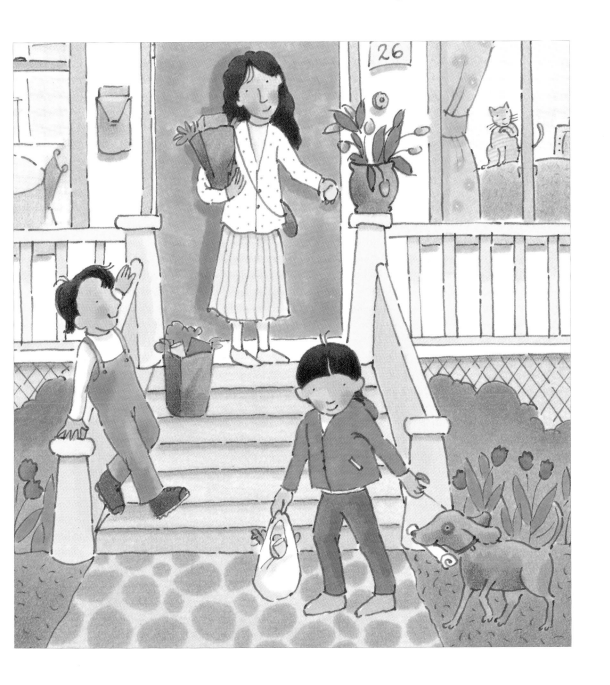

My brother and I are staying with
Aunt Carmen.

We are having fun.

But at night we don't have any fun at all—

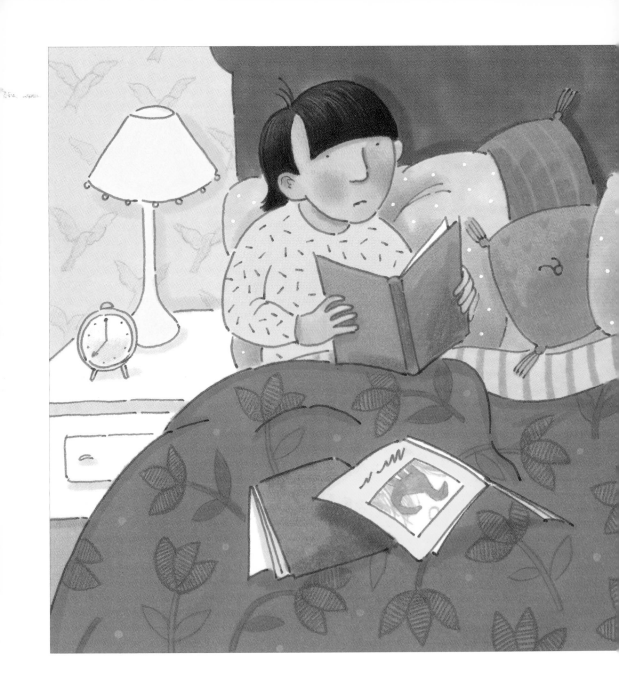

My brother and I have to share a bed.

"Stop bumping me!" I told Edgar.
"I didn't bump you," he said.

And I said, "Well, somebody bumped me."
And he said, "It wasn't me!"

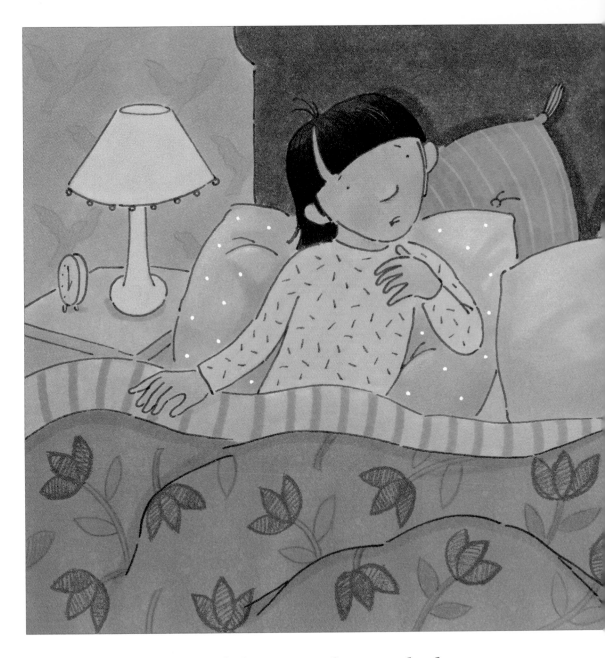

After a while, something poked me.
"Stop poking me!" I told Edgar.
"I didn't poke you," he said.

10

And I said, "Well, somebody poked me."
And he said, "It wasn't me!"

After a while, something shoved me.
"Stop shoving me!" I told Edgar.
"I didn't shove you," he said.

And I said, "Well, somebody shoved me."
And he said, "It wasn't me!"

After a while, something tugged at the covers.
"Stop tugging the covers!" I told Edgar.
"I didn't tug them," he said.

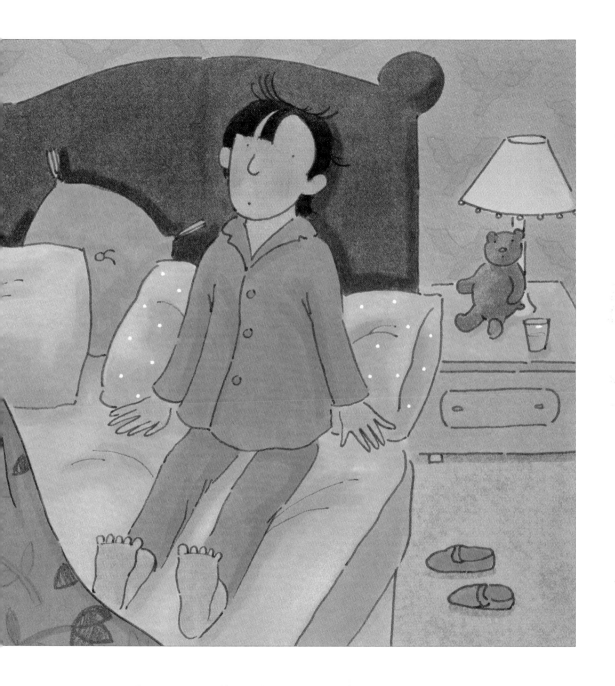

And I said, "Well, somebody tugged them."
And he said, "It wasn't me!"

"I'm tired of this," said Edgar.
"I'm going to sleep on the couch."
Edgar left. I had the bed to myself.

After a while, I heard snoring.
"Stop snoring!" I told Edgar.
But nobody said, "I didn't snore."

Then I remembered. Edgar was on
the couch.

So who snored?

I turned on the light.

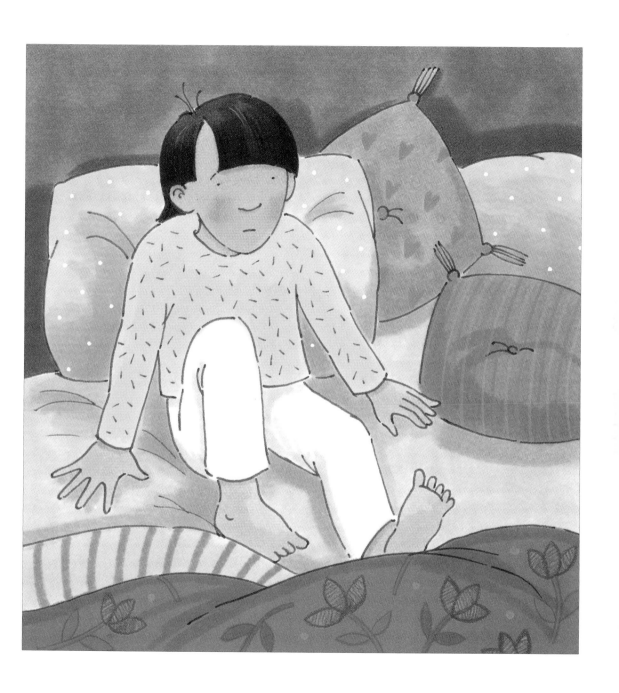

I pushed back the covers.

What did I see? Aunt Carmen's dog Woof!

Was it Woof who bumped me?

Was it Woof who poked me?

Was it Woof who shoved me?

Was it Woof who tugged the covers?

23

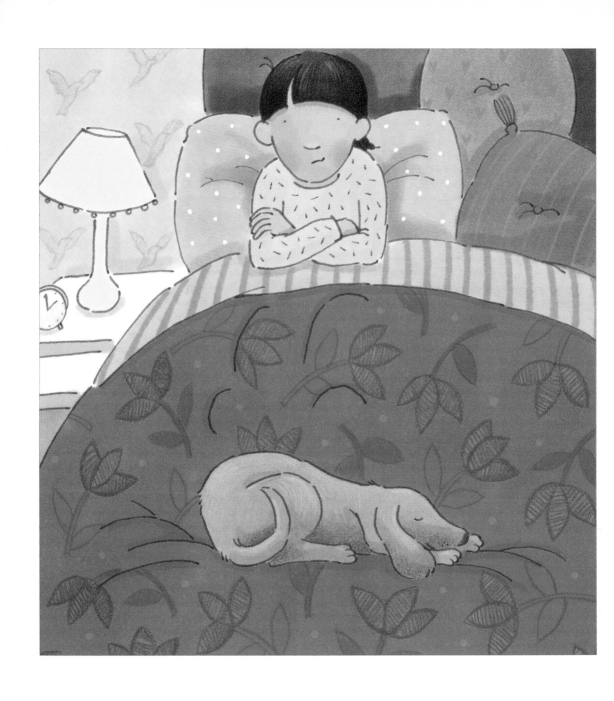

I guess I'll never know.